Indian Cobra

by Grace Hansen

Abdo ASIAN ANIMALS Kids

Abdo Kids Jumbo is an Imprint of Abdo Kids
abdobooks.com

abdobooks.com

Published by Abdo Kids, a division of ABDO, P.O. Box 398166, Minneapolis, Minnesota 55439.

Printed in the United States of America, North Mankato, Minnesota.

102020

012021

THIS BOOK CONTAINS RECYCLED MATERIALS

Photo Credits: Alamy, Getty Images, iStock, Minden Pictures, Science Source, Shutterstock

Production Contributors: Teddy Borth, Jennie Forsberg, Grace Hansen
Design Contributors: Dorothy Toth, Pakou Moua

Library of Congress Control Number: 2020910694

Publisher's Cataloging-in-Publication Data

Names: Hansen, Grace, author.

Title: Indian cobra / by Grace Hansen

Description: Minneapolis, Minnesota : Abdo Kids, 2021 | Series: Asian animals | Includes online resources and index.

Identifiers: ISBN 9781098205959 (lib. bdg.) | ISBN 9781098206512 (ebook) | ISBN 9781098206796 (Read-to-Me ebook)

Subjects: LCSH: Cobras--Juvenile literature. | Poisonous snakes--Juvenile literature. | Rain forest animals--Juvenile literature. | Animals--Juvenile literature. | Asia--Juvenile literature. | Endangered species--Juvenile literature.

Classification: DDC 597.964--dc23

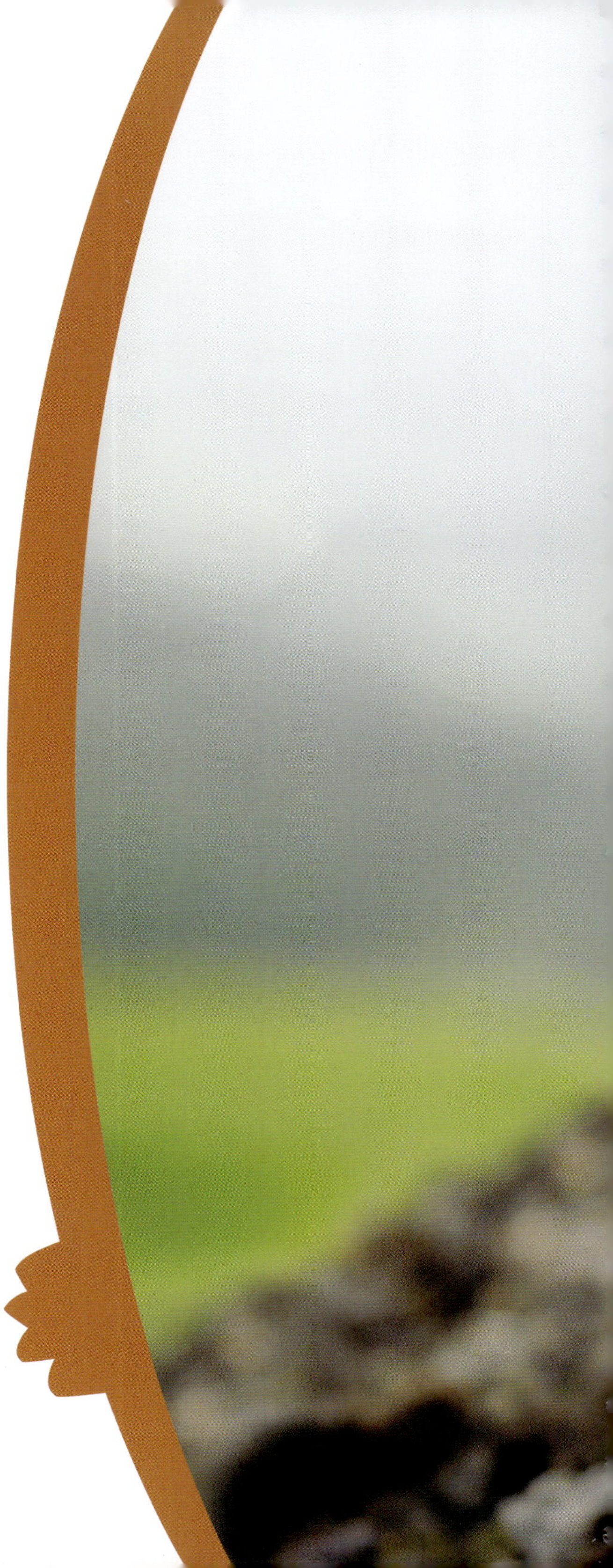

Table of Contents

Indian Cobra Habitat

Indian cobras can be found throughout most of India. But they also live in other countries, like Pakistan, Sri Lanka and Nepal.

Asia
Pakistan
Nepal
India
Bangladesh
Sri Lanka
N
E
S
W

Indian cobras live in many different habitats. They can be found in dense forests and open plains. They find good hiding spots, like hollow trees and rock piles.

Body

Indian cobras are around 5 feet (1.5 m) long. They are covered in smooth scales.

Their scales can be tan, brown, and black in color. The snakes also have a speckled pattern.

The Indian cobra is easily recognized by its **hood**. When threatened, the snake rears up. It pushes its neck out to form the hood.

The **hood** makes the snake look bigger. This protects it from **predators**.

If the **hood** does not work, the Indian cobra is not afraid to strike. An Indian cobra's **venom** is deadly.

Food & Hunting

Indian cobras also use their **venom** for hunting. Their bite paralyzes **prey**. Then they eat the prey whole.

Baby Indian Cobras

Females lay 12 to 20 eggs in a tree or in the ground. Mothers protect their eggs. The eggs hatch after about 50 days.

More Facts

- The Indian cobra is called an Indian spectacled cobra. This is because of the large black spots with white rings on the cobra's **hood**.
- Indian cobras are usually slow to bite. They will first rear up and hiss sharply to warn **predators**.
- The Indian cobra is the favorite kind of cobra used by snake charmers. The snake sways to the motion of the charmer's musical instrument.

Glossary

hood – a cobra's body part that is formed by many elongated ribs that extend the looser skin on the neck outwards.

predator – an animal that hunts other animals for food.

prey – an animal hunted by another animal for food.

venom – the poison that certain snakes, insects, scorpions, and other animals produce. Venom is put into prey by biting or stinging.

Index